STORY BY
OSCAR WILDE

ILLUSTRATIONS BY
CHRIS BEATRICE

MUSICAL ADAPTION BY
DAN GOELLER

NARRATION BY
MARTIN JARVIS

noteworthy books

Published by Noteworthy Books
Art Design and Layout by Pam Latour

_____

Library of Congress Cataloging-in-Publication Data

THE SELFISH GIANT
by Oscar Wilde, 1854–1900
Musical Adaptation by Dan Goeller
Illustrations by Chris Beatrice
Narration by Martin Jarvis

Summary: After the Selfish Giant builds a wall to keep the village children from
playing in his garden, he finds his beautiful garden trapped in an endless winter.

[1. Fairy tales – Juvenile Fiction.   2. English Short Stories – Irish Authors.
3. Symphonic Music – for children]
I. Beatrice, Chris, ill.   II. Title

Library of Congress Control Number: 2010938561

_____

ISBN: 978-0-9830038-0-9

10 9 8 7 6 5 4 3 2

Printed in China

Noteworthy Books
Sioux Falls, SD

This edition is an unabridged, unedited reproduction of the original Oscar Wilde text. It is slightly different from the
narration on the audio recording and may contain punctuation and spelling that differs from modern American usage.

Please visit us at www.SelfishGiantMusic.com

Every afternoon, as they were coming from school, the children used to go and play in the Giant's garden.

It was a large lovely garden, with soft green grass. Here and there over the grass stood beautiful flowers like stars, and there were twelve peach-trees that in the spring-time broke out into delicate blossoms of pink and pearl, and in the autumn bore rich fruit. The birds sat on the trees and sang so sweetly that the children used to stop their games in order to listen to them. "How happy we are here!" they cried to each other.

One day the Giant came back. He had been to visit his friend the Cornish ogre, and had stayed with him for seven years. After the seven years were over he had said all that he had to say, for his conversation was limited, and he determined to return to his own castle. When he arrived he saw the children playing in the garden.

"What are you doing here?" he cried in a very gruff voice, and the children ran away.

"My own garden is my own garden," said the Giant; "any one can understand that, and I will allow nobody to play in it but myself."

So he built a high wall all round it, and put up a notice-board.

TRESPASSERS WILL
BE PROSECUTED

He was a very selfish Giant.

The poor children had now nowhere to play. They tried to play on the road, but the road was very dusty and full of hard stones, and they did not like it. They used to wander round the high wall when their lessons were over, and talk about the beautiful garden inside. "How happy we were there," they said to each other.

＊ ＊ ＊

Then the Spring came, and all over the country there were little blossoms and little birds. Only in the garden of the Selfish Giant it was still winter. The birds did not care to sing in it as there were no children, and the trees forgot to blossom. Once a beautiful flower put its head out from the grass, but when it saw the notice-board it was so sorry for the children that it slipped back into the ground again, and went off to sleep.

The only people who were pleased were the Snow and the Frost. "Spring has forgotten this garden," they cried, "so we will live here all the year round." The Snow covered up the grass with her great white cloak, and the Frost painted all the trees silver. Then they invited the North Wind to stay with them, and he came. He was wrapped in furs, and he roared all day about the garden, and blew the chimney-pots down. "This is a delightful spot," he said, "we must ask the Hail on a visit." So the Hail came. Every day for three hours he rattled on the roof of the castle till he broke most of the slates, and then he ran round and round the garden as fast as he could go. He was dressed in grey, and his breath was like ice.

"I cannot understand why the Spring is so late in coming," said the Selfish Giant, as he sat at the window and looked out at his cold white garden; "I hope there will be a change in the weather."

But the Spring never came, nor the Summer. The Autumn gave golden fruit to every garden, but to the Giant's garden she gave none. "He is too selfish," she said. So it was always Winter there, and the North Wind, and the Hail, and the Frost, and the Snow danced about through the trees.

One morning the Giant was lying awake in bed when he heard some lovely music. It sounded so sweet to his ears that he thought it must be the King's musicians passing by. It was really only a little linnet singing outside his window, but it was so long since he had heard a bird sing in his garden that it seemed to him to be the most beautiful music in the world. Then the Hail stopped dancing over his head, and the North Wind ceased roaring, and a delicious perfume came to him through the open casement. "I believe the Spring has come at last," said the Giant; and he jumped out of bed and looked out.

What did he see?

He saw a most wonderful sight. Through a little hole in the wall the children had crept in, and they were sitting in the branches of the trees. In every tree that he could see there was a little child. And the trees were so glad to have the children back again that they had covered themselves with blossoms, and were waving their arms gently above the children's heads. The birds were flying about and twittering with delight, and the flowers were looking up through the green grass and laughing. It was a lovely scene, only in one corner it was still winter. It was the farthest corner of the garden, and in it was standing a little boy. He was so small that he could not reach up to the branches of the tree, and he was wandering all round it, crying bitterly.

The poor tree was still quite covered with frost and snow, and the North Wind was blowing and roaring above it. "Climb up! little boy," said the Tree, and it bent its branches down as low as it could; but the boy was too tiny.

And the Giant's heart melted as he looked out. "How selfish I have been!" he said; "now I know why the Spring would not come here. I will put that poor little boy on the top of the tree, and then I will knock down the wall, and my garden shall be the children's playground for ever and ever." He was really very sorry for what he had done.

So he crept downstairs and opened the front door quite softly, and went out into the garden. But when the children saw him they were so frightened that they all ran away, and the garden became winter again. Only the little boy did not run, for his eyes were so full of tears that he did not see the Giant coming. And the Giant stole up behind him and took him gently in his hand, and put him up into the tree. And the tree broke at once into blossom, and the birds came and sang on it, and the little boy stretched out his two arms and flung them round the Giant's neck, and kissed him.

And the other children, when they saw
that the Giant was not wicked any longer, came
running back, and with them came the Spring. "It
is your garden now, little children," said the Giant,
and he took a great axe and knocked down the
wall. And when the people were going to market
at twelve o'clock they found the Giant playing
with the children in the most beautiful garden
they had ever seen.

All day long they played, and in the evening
they came to the Giant to bid him good-bye.

"But where is your little companion?" he said:
"the boy I put into the tree." The Giant loved him
the best because he had kissed him.

"We don't know," answered the children; "he
has gone away."

"You must tell him to be sure and come here
to-morrow," said the Giant. But the children said
that they did not know where he lived, and had
never seen him before; and the Giant felt very sad.

very afternoon, when school was over, the children came and played with the Giant. But the little boy whom the Giant loved was never seen again. The Giant was very kind to all the children, yet he longed for his first little friend, and often spoke of him. "How I would like to see him!" he used to say.

Years went over, and the Giant grew very old and feeble. He could not play about any more, so he sat in a huge armchair, and watched the children at their games, and admired his garden. "I have many beautiful flowers," he said; "but the children are the most beautiful flowers of all."

One winter morning he
looked out of his window as he
was dressing. He did not hate the
Winter now, for he knew that it was
merely the Spring asleep, and that
the flowers were resting.

Suddenly he rubbed his eyes
in wonder, and looked and looked.
It certainly was a marvellous sight.
In the farthest corner of the garden
was a tree quite covered with lovely
white blossoms. Its branches were
all golden, and silver fruit hung
down from them, and underneath it
stood the little boy he had loved.

Downstairs ran the Giant in
great joy, and out into the garden. He
hastened across the grass, and came near
to the child. And when he came quite
close his face grew red with anger, and he
said, "Who hath dared to wound thee?"
For on the palms of the child's hands
were the prints of two nails, and the
prints of two nails were on the little feet.

"Who hath dared to wound thee?"
cried the Giant; "tell me, that I may take
my big sword and slay him."

"Nay!" answered the child; "but
these are the wounds of Love."

"Who art thou?" said the Giant, and a strange awe fell on him, and he knelt before the little child.

And the child smiled on the Giant, and said to him, "You let me play once in your garden, to-day you shall come with me to my garden, which is Paradise."

And when the children ran in that afternoon, they found the Giant lying dead under the tree, all covered with white blossoms.

ABOUT THE AUTHOR

Classic Irish author Oscar Wilde (1854–1900) once told an interviewer, "It is the duty of every father to write fairy tales for his children."[1] Wilde took his own advice by telling fairy tales to his sons, Cyril and Vyvyan. These tales, including "The Selfish Giant," were published in an 1888 collection, *The Happy Prince and Other Tales*. Cyril once asked his father why he had tears in his eyes when he told them the story of "The Selfish Giant." Wilde replied that really beautiful things always made him cry.[2]

In addition to fairy tales, Oscar Wilde also wrote plays, essays, and the classic novel, *The Picture of Dorian Gray*. He is most remembered today as a playwright, especially for *An Ideal Husband* and *The Importance of Being Earnest*, his most famous comedies.

ABOUT THE MUSIC

Dan Goeller is the composer and conductor of the music heard on *The Selfish Giant* CD. Because he remembered hearing *The Selfish Giant* as a child, he read Wilde's story to his young daughters. Like Wilde, the beauty of the story brought tears to Goeller's eyes. He decided to adapt the story for orchestra and narrator. First, Goeller divided the story into sections, much like the script for a play. Then he decided where the music would underscore the narrated story and where it would capture the story's action without the words.

Once Goeller decided how the music would interact with the story, he listed all the characters. He paired orchestra instruments with the characters, making sure each instrument imitated the personality or sound of each character. For example, the flute and the piccolo imitate the birds that "sang so sweetly." For the Giant, Goeller chose the largest instrument in the brass family: the tuba. The oboe portrays the wistful flower that pokes its head up from the grass.

In addition to the timbre, or sound, of the instruments, Goeller also used special techniques to portray story elements. For example, the tremolos, the shimmering sound of the violins, imitate the delicate falling of the Snow's white cloak over the grass. For Jack Frost's brush painting the trees silver, listen for the fast flurry of clarinets. The clatter of hail can be heard in the plucking of the strings, a technique called pizzicato. The North Wind roars about in the smeary slides of the trombone section.

To learn more about *The Selfish Giant*, the music, or the creators who brought this story to life, visit www.SelfishGiantMusic.com for videos, games, and more.

[1] Hyde, Montgomery H. Oscar Wilde: A Biography. London: Eyre Methuen, 1976, p. 106.
[2] Ibid. p. 107